Franklin Is Lost

For Wesley – PB

With thanks to Lois Keddy and her family – BC

Franklin

Franklin and the Franklin characters are trademarks of Kids Can Press Ltd.

Kids Can Press is a Nelvana company.

ISBN 0-439-35501-X

12 11 10 9 8 7 6 5 4 3 2 1   1 2 3 4 5 6/0
Printed in Singapore   46

First Scholastic printing, February 1993
First Scholastic miniature edition printing, October 2001

Franklin Is Lost

Written by Paulette Bourgeois
Illustrated by Brenda Clark

SCHOLASTIC INC.

New York   Toronto   London   Auckland   Sydney
Mexico City   New Delhi   Hong Kong   Buenos Aires

FRANKLIN could slide down a river bank. He could count forwards and backwards. He could zip zippers and button buttons. He could even walk to Bear's house all by himself. But Franklin was not allowed to go into the woods alone.

One day Franklin said, "I'm going to play at Bear's house."

"All right," said Franklin's mother. "But be home for dinner by six o'clock." She showed him the time with the hands of the clock. "And Franklin," she warned, "don't go into the woods alone."

Franklin raced down the path, over the bridge and across the berry patch.

Bear was there. Fox was there. Goose and Otter were there.

"I'm here," huffed Franklin. "What are you playing?"

"Hide and seek," shouted his friends. "And you're It."

Franklin started counting. Hide and seek was his favorite game. He wasn't very fast but he was very clever. He knew Bear always hid in the berry patch.

Franklin looked around. He saw a shaggy paw swipe at a branch of berries.

"I see you, Bear," he called.

Franklin spotted feathers and fur under the bridge.
"I see you, Goose. I see you, Otter," he called.

Only Fox was left to find. Franklin walked this
way and that. He looked into bushes and searched
under logs. He walked along the path and over
the bridge and without even thinking, he walked
right into the woods.

He looked into burrows and all around trees.
Franklin searched everywhere but he couldn't
find Fox.

Fox wasn't in the woods at all. He was hiding inside Bear's house. After awhile he shouted, "Can't catch me!"

But Franklin couldn't hear him. He was too far away.

"Where's Franklin?" asked Fox.

Nobody knew.

They waited a long time. Bear's tummy grumbled. Finally, Goose said, "It's almost six o'clock. Franklin must have hurried home for supper."

"Of course," they said, and off they went.

At Franklin's house, the clock struck six. Franklin's parents were annoyed. Their supper was ready.

By half-past six, they were worried and went looking for Franklin.

Franklin's father searched along the path. "Franklin," he called. "Where are you?"

Franklin's mother talked to his friends.
"Where's Franklin?" she asked Bear.

"Where's Franklin?" she asked Otter and Goose.
"Where's Franklin?" she asked Fox.
Nobody knew. Now they were worried, too.

It was getting dark. Franklin turned one way and then another. Every tree looked the same. Every rock looked the same. He couldn't find the path.

"I'm lost," said Franklin in a tiny little voice.

He couldn't remember which way he had come. He didn't know which way to go. He was tired and frightened and all alone. Franklin curled up in his small dark shell and waited. Somebody would come. Sometime. Wouldn't they?

Dark shadows flitted across the rocks.

"Who's there?" whispered Franklin. But no one answered because it was the clouds blowing across the face of the moon.

"Whoo. Whoo."

"Who's there?" whispered Franklin. But no one answered because it was Owl far, far away.

"Whewwww. Whewwww."

"Who's there?" whispered Franklin. But no one answered because it was the wind whistling through the trees.

Franklin tried to sleep, but every sound made him jump.

He was humming himself a little tune when he heard: "Crick, crack, crick, crack, crick, crack, squish."

"Who's there?" whispered Franklin. But no one answered.

Then Franklin heard a new sound. It sounded like someone calling his name.

He heard it again.

"Here I am! Here I am!" Franklin shouted over and over.

CRICK CRACK, CRICK CRACK, CRICK CRACK,
SQUISH. Franklin's parents came over the knoll.
"There you are!" They hugged him and kissed
him and held him tight.
"We were so worried," said Franklin's father.

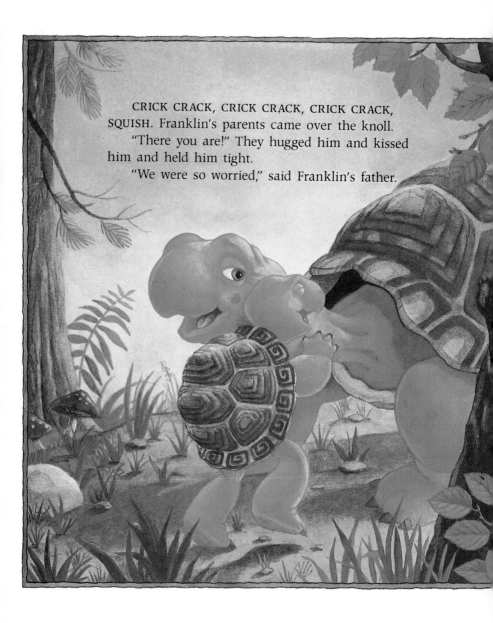

"You were told not to go into the woods alone," scolded his mother.

"It wasn't on purpose," sniffled Franklin. "I was looking for Fox and I forgot."

"Well, thank goodness you're safe," said Franklin's parents.

They found the path and walked all the way home. Their supper was still warm in the oven. After two helpings of everything, Franklin had something important to say.

"I'm sorry. I promise I'll never go into the woods alone again."

"Even if Fox hides there?" asked his mother.

"Even if Bear hides there?" asked his father.

"Even if everybody hides there!" said Franklin.

It was half-past bedtime. Franklin crawled into his warm, safe shell.

"Good night, dear," said his parents.
But no one answered because Franklin
had fallen fast asleep.